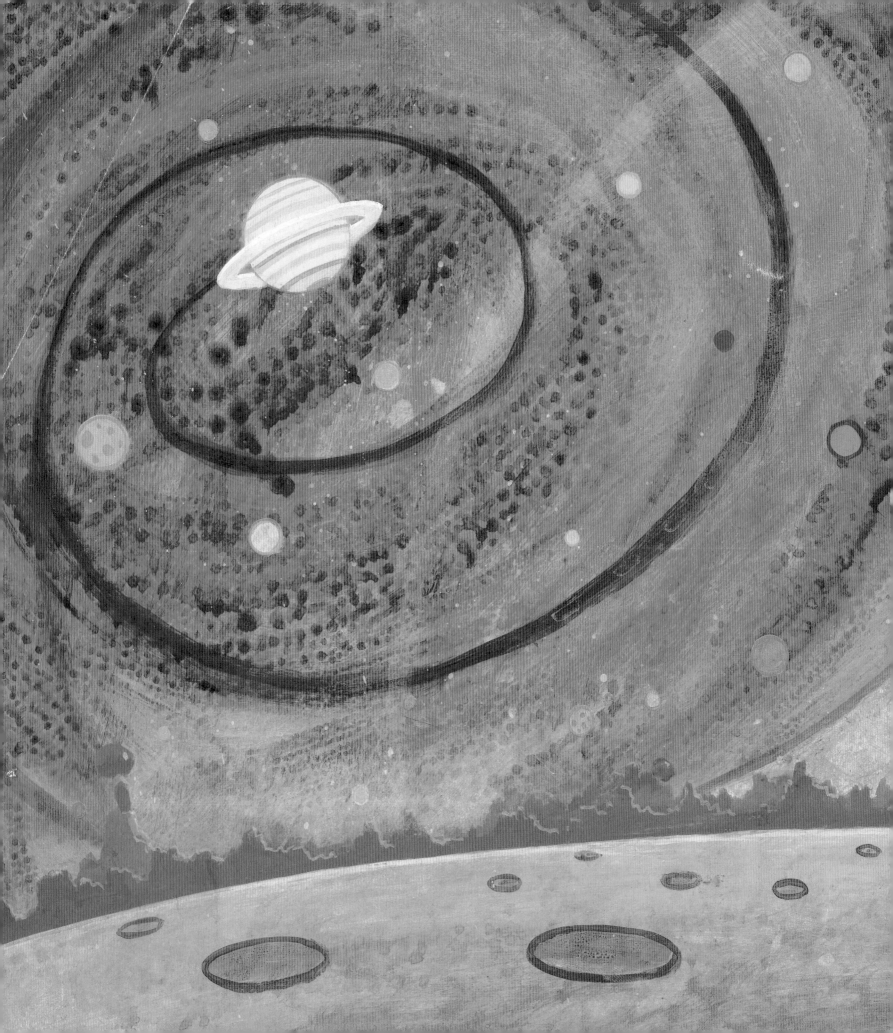

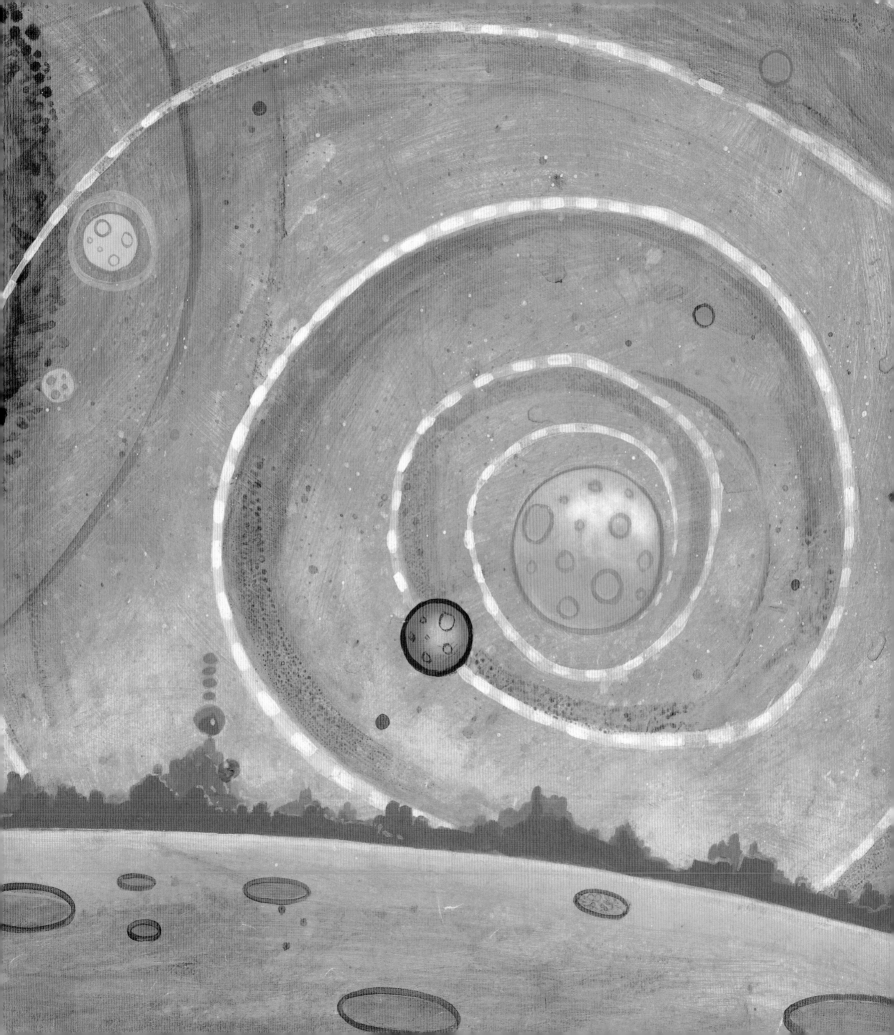

An meinen lieben Onkel Wolfgang mit viel Liebe
C.F.

For Ava x
R.J.

First published in 2016 by Scholastic Children's Books
Euston House, 24 Eversholt Street
London NW1 1DB
a division of Scholastic Ltd
www.scholastic.co.uk
London ~ New York ~ Toronto ~ Sydney ~ Auckland
Mexico City ~ New Delhi ~ Hong Kong

Text copyright © 2016 Claire Freedman
Illustrations copyright © 2016 Russell Julian

ISBN 978 1407 15267 7

SCHOLASTIC

ASTRO

THE ROBOT DOG

Claire Freedman   Russell Julian

Young Astro was a robot dog,
He lived in space, on Planet Xog.
His owner, Zak, an alien boy,
Bought Astro as a robot toy.

The dog was built from metal parts,
With knobs to push, for stops and starts.
He did as all good robots do –
Whatever he was programmed to!

In space, life was computer-run,
But somehow they forgot the fun.
Zak sighed, "I wish Astro was real,
But robot dogs aren't built to feel!"

One day, on Zak's computer screen,
A message flashed up,
              neon green:

Urgent request from Space-Probe Log.

We need to use your robot dog!

He's been selected for a task.

No questions answered – please don't ask!

A jet car picked them up and flew
At sonic speed to Space H.Q.
The mission: visit Humankind,
Then report back with what you find!

They gave Astro a space-linked phone,
A collar with a radar cone.
Then in his spaceship, safely strapped,

whoosh!

Down to Planet Earth he zapped!

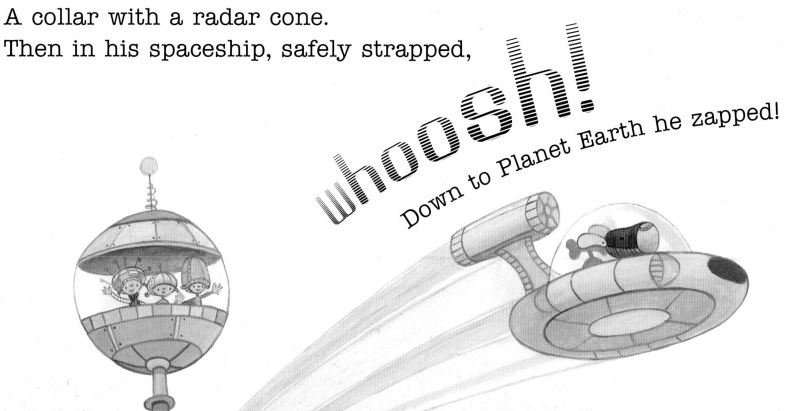

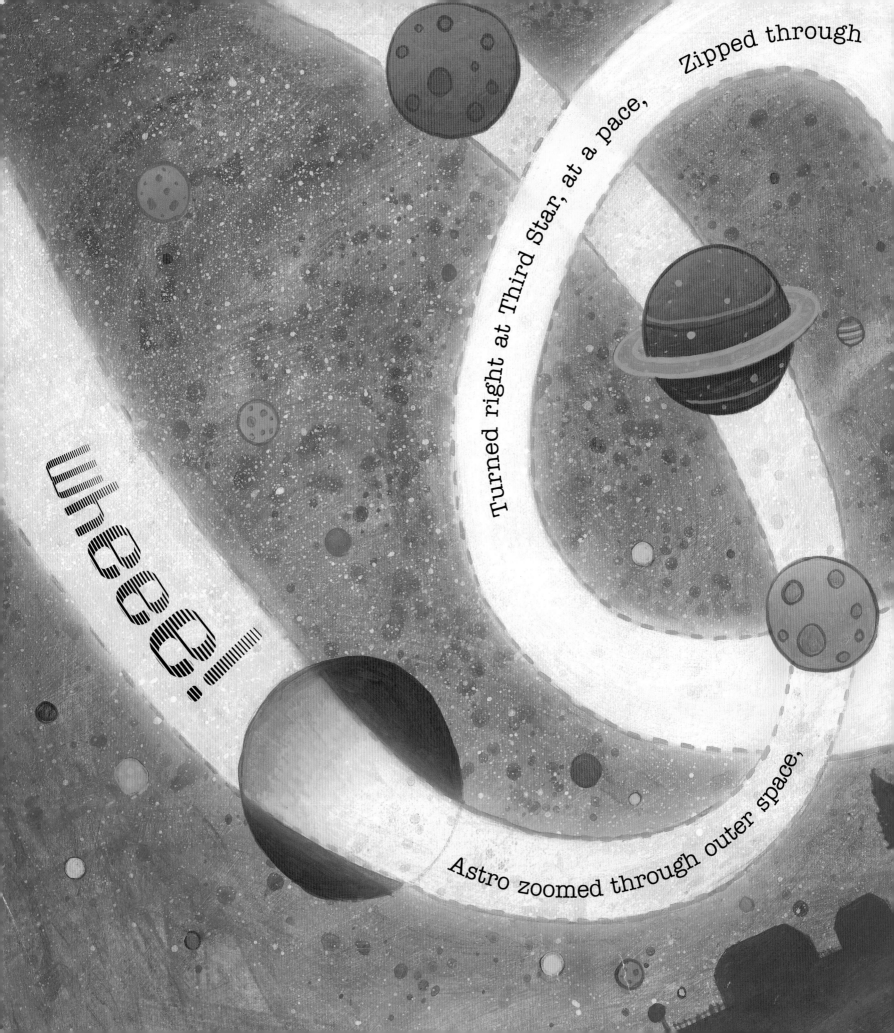

Wheee!

Astro zoomed through outer space,

Turned right at Third Star, at a pace,

Zipped through

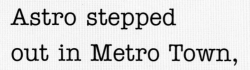

Astro stepped
out in Metro Town,

"What now?" he wondered,
with a frown.
His collar then bleeped,
"Time to meet,
This boy who's walking
down the street!"

So bravely, Astro marched straight up,
"Hey!" gasped the boy, "A robot pup!
Someone has left him all alone,
He looks so lost, I'll take him home!"

As Astro watched the boy each day,
He saw him laugh and climb and play.

Boy's life was not
computer-run,

But, strangely,
it seemed lots of fun!

At night Astro sent data back,
"Earth is SO different, please tell Zak.
We splashed in streams and kicked a ball,
It's not like life on Xog at all."

The boy took Astro to the park,
They played great games till it grew dark.

Thought Astro, this is fun to do,
Would Zak like playing Earth games too?

That night, curled up with Boy in bed,
Strange thoughts whirled round in Astro's head,

"Although I'm made from steel and tin,
I'm feeling soft and warm within."

But then a stronger feeling came,
A deeper longing, not the same,
"I care for Boy but he's not Zak,
I miss Zak more – I must go back!"

The summons home arrived next day:

Return to Hog, please, no delay!
Your Travel Pod arrives at eight,
The mission's over — don't be late!

Astro showed Boy his space-age phone,
His collar with a radar cone.
He said, "I'm sad to leave this place,
But my home is with Zak, in space.

Although I'm just a metal toy,
I've learnt to feel – so thank you Boy!"

Boy smiled and nodded, "Don't be sad,
You found your heart, I'm really glad.
Go home to Zak, where you belong,
To stay with us would just be wrong!"

WHOOSH!

Down the Pod dropped, from the sky,
Just time to hug and say goodbye.
"Take this with you!" Boy shouted out,
"Show Zak what football's all about!"

The Pod docked home, Astro was back,
He barked with joy at seeing Zak.

Huge crowds had come to see the dog
Who'd been to Earth, and back to Xog!

At long last they were all alone,
Just Zak and Astro, on their own.

"What was Earth like?" Zak asked that night.
"Like this," and Astro hugged Zak tight.